Jack & Jill
& other
Nursery Rhymes

PaRragon

Bath · New York · Singapore · Hong Kong · Cologne · Delhi · Melbourne

JACK AND JILL

Jack and Jill went up the hill
  To fetch a pail of water;
Jack fell down and broke his crown,
  And Jill came tumbling after.

Up Jack got, and home did trot,
  As fast as he could caper,
Went to bed to mend his head
  With vinegar and brown paper.

JACK, JACK, THE BREAD'S A-BURNING

Jack, Jack, the bread's a-burning,
All to a cinder;
If you don't come and fetch it out
We'll throw it through the window.

JACK AND GUY

Jack and Guy
Went out in the rye,
And they found a little boy with one black eye.
Come, says Jack, let's knock him on the head.
No, says Guy, let's buy him some bread;
You buy one loaf and I'll buy two,
And we'll bring him up as other folk do.

HERE WE GO ROUND THE MULBERRY BUSH

Here we go round the mulberry bush,
The mulberry bush, the mulberry bush,
Here we go round the mulberry bush,
On a cold and frosty morning.

This is the way we wash our hands,
Wash our hands, wash our hands,
This is the way we wash our hands,
On a cold and frosty morning.

Here we go round the mulberry bush,
The mulberry bush, the mulberry bush,
Here we go round the mulberry bush,
On a cold and frosty morning.

This is the way we wash our clothes,
Wash our clothes, wash our clothes,
This is the way we wash our clothes,
On a cold and frosty morning.

Here we go round the mulberry bush,
The mulberry bush, the mulberry bush,
Here we go round the mulberry bush,
On a cold and frosty morning.

This is the way we go to school,
We go to school, we go to school,
This is the way we go to school,
On a cold and frosty morning.

Here we go round the mulberry bush,
The mulberry bush, the mulberry bush,
Here we go round the mulberry bush,
On a cold and frosty morning.

ROBIN AND RICHARD

Robin and Richard were two pretty men;
They laid in bed till the clock struck ten;
Then up starts Robin and looks at the sky,
Oh! brother Richard, the sun's very high:

The bull's in the barn threshing the corn,
The cock's on the dunghill blowing his horn,
The cat's at the fire frying of fish,
The dog's in the pantry breaking his dish.

LITTLE TOMMY TITTLEMOUSE

Little Tommy Tittlemouse
Lived in a little house;
He caught fishes
In other men's ditches.

SEE-SAW, MARGERY DAW

See-saw, Margery Daw,
Jack shall have a new master;
He shall have but a penny a day,
Because he can't work any faster.

FIVE LITTLE MONKEYS

Five little monkeys walked along the shore;
One went a-sailing,
Then there were four.
Four little monkeys climbed up a tree;
One of them tumbled down,
Then there were three.
Three little monkeys found a pot of glue;
One got stuck in it,
Then there were two.
Two little monkeys found a currant bun;
One ran away with it,
Then there was one.
One little monkey cried all afternoon,
So they put him in an aeroplane
And sent him to the moon.

THREE CHILDREN

Three children sliding on the ice
   Upon a summer's day,
As it fell out, they all fell in,
   The rest they ran away.

Now had these children been at home,
   Or sliding on dry ground,
Ten thousand pounds to one penny
   They had not all been drowned.

You parents all that children have,
   And you that have got none,
If you would have them safe abroad,
   Pray keep them safe at home.

PEASE-PUDDING HOT

Pease-pudding hot,
  Pease-pudding cold,
Pease-pudding in the pot,
  Nine days old.
Some like it hot,
  Some like it cold,
Some like it in the pot,
  Nine days old.

THE MAN IN THE MOON

The man in the moon,
  Came tumbling down,
And asked his way to Norwich.
  He went by the south,
  And burnt his mouth
With supping cold pease-porridge.

GOOSEY, GOOSEY, GANDER

Goosey, goosey, gander,
  Whither shall I wander,
Upstairs, and downstairs,
  And in my lady's chamber.
There I met an old man,
  Who would not say his prayers,
I took him by his left leg
  And threw him down the stairs.

DAFFY-DOWN-DILLY

Daffy-
Down-
Dilly
has come
up to
town

In a
yellow
petticoat
and a
green
gown.

TIGGY-TOUCHWOOD

Tiggy-tiggy-touchwood, my black hen,
She lays eggs for gentlemen,
Sometimes nine and sometimes ten,
Tiggy-tiggy-touchwood, my black hen.

I HAD A LITTLE HEN

I had a little hen, the prettiest ever seen,
She washed me the dishes, and kept the house clean:
She went to the mill to fetch me some flour,
She brought it home in less than an hour;
She baked me my bread, she brewed me my ale,
She sat by the fire and told many a fine tale.

MRS. HEN

Chook, chook, chook, chook, chook,
   Good morning, Mrs. Hen.
How many chickens have you got?
   Madam, I've got ten.

Four of them are yellow,
   And four of them are brown,
And two of them are speckled red,
   The nicest in the town.

THE KEY OF THE KINGDOM

This is the key of the kingdom:
In that kingdom is a city,
In that city is a town,
In that town there is a street,
In that street there winds a lane,
In that lane there is a yard,
In that yard there is a house,
In that house there waits a room,
In that room there is a bed,
On that bed there is a basket,
　A basket of flowers.

Flowers in the basket,
Basket on the bed,
Bed in the chamber,
Chamber in the house,
House in the weedy yard,
Yard in the winding lane,
Lane in the broad street,
Street in the high town,
Town in the city,
City in the kingdom:
  This is the key of the kingdom.
  Of the kingdom this is the key.

THREE LITTLE KITTENS

Three little kittens they lost their mittens,
    And they began to cry,
Oh, mother dear, we sadly fear
    That we have lost our mittens.
What! lost your mittens, you naughty kittens!
    Then you shall have no pie.
    Mee-ow, mee-ow, mee-ow.
    No, you shall have no pie.

The three little kittens they found their mittens,
    And they began to cry,
Oh, mother dear, see here, see here,
    For we have found our mittens.
Put on your mittens, you silly kittens,
    And you shall have some pie.
    Purr-r, purr-r, purr-r,
    Oh, let us have some pie.

The three little kittens put on their mittens,
    And soon ate up the pie;
Oh, mother dear, we greatly fear
    That we have soiled our mittens.
What! soiled your mittens, you naughty kittens!
    Then they began to sigh.
    Mee-ow, mee-ow, mee-ow.
    Then they began to sigh.

The three little kittens they washed their mittens,
    And hung them out to dry;
Oh! mother dear, do you not hear
    That we have washed our mittens?
What! washed your mittens, then you're good kittens,
    But I smell a rat close by.
    Mee-ow, mee-ow, mee-ow.
    We smell a rat close by.

SOLOMON GRUNDY

Solomon Grundy,
Born on Monday,
Christened on Tuesday,
Married on
Wednesday,
Sick on Thursday,
Worse on Friday,
Died on Saturday,
Buried on Sunday,
That was the end
Of Solomon Grundy.

OLD KING COLE

Old King Cole
Was a merry old soul,
And a merry old soul was he;
He called for his pipe,
And he called for his bowl,
And he called for his fiddlers three.
Every fiddler had a fine fiddle,
And a very fine fiddle had he;
Twee tweedle dee, tweedle dee, went the fiddlers,
   Very merry men are we;
   Oh there's none so rare
   As can compare
With King Cole and his fiddlers three.

THE MAN IN THE WILDERNESS

The man in the Wilderness asked me,
How many strawberries grew in the sea?
I answered him as I thought good,
As many red herrings as grew in the wood.

A PEANUT SAT ON THE RAILROAD TRACK

A peanut sat on the railroad track,
His heart was all a-flutter;
Along came a train—the 9:15—
Toot, toot, peanut butter!

THE QUEEN OF HEARTS

The Queen of Hearts, she made some tarts,
  All on a summer's day;
The Knave of Hearts, he stole the tarts,
  And took them clean away.

The King of Hearts called for the tarts,
  And beat the Knave full sore;
The Knave of Hearts brought back the tarts,
  And vowed he'd steal no more.

A FACE GAME

Here sits the Lord Mayor;	*Forehead*
Here sit his two men;	*Eyes*
Here sits the cock;	*Right cheek*
Here sits the hen;	*Left cheek*
Here sit the little chickens;	*Tip of nose*
Here they run in,	*Mouth*
Chinchopper, chinchopper,	
Chinchopper, chin!	*Chuck the chin*

MY GRANDMOTHER SENT ME

My grandmother sent me a new-fashioned three cornered cambric country cut handkerchief. Not an old-fashioned three cornered cambric country cut handkerchief, but a new-fashioned three cornered cambric country cut handkerchief.

ROBERT ROWLEY

Robert Rowley rolled a round roll round,
A round roll Robert Rowley rolled round;
Where rolled the round roll Robert Rowley
 rolled round?

OLD JOHN MUDDLECOMBE

Old John Muddlecombe lost his cap,
He couldn't find it anywhere, the poor old chap.
He walked down the High Street, and everybody said,
"Silly John Muddlecombe, you've got it on your head!"

POOR OLD ROBINSON CRUSOE

Poor old Robinson Crusoe!
Poor old Robinson Crusoe!
  They made him a coat
  Of an old nanny goat,

  I wonder how they could do so!
With a ring a ting tang,
And a ring a ting tang,
  Poor old Robinson Crusoe!

BAT, BAT

Bat, Bat, come under my hat,
  And I'll give you a slice of bacon,
And when I bake I'll give you a cake,
  If I am not mistaken.